Snot Rocket

and the
Weapon of MATH
Destruction

Written by Ryan Stygar
Illustrations by Garrett Dare

SNOT ROCKET
Book 1: The Weapon of Math Destruction

ISBN-13: 978-1722201791

Cover art and illustrations by Garrett Dare

Snot Rocket

and the
Weapon of MATH
Destruction

Chapter 1: Trouble in Space

The astronauts aboard the Space Station were the best of the best. Each was selected not only for their skills in math, science, and space flight, but also for their courage. Their names were Yung Li, from China, Igor Popov, from Russia, and Commander Patti Steal, from the United States.

Yung Li pushed away from his computer and floated in zero gravity. "All this work is making me thirsty. Hey Igor, pass me another packet of Tang."

The Russian astronaut chuckled. "You've had four today already! Perhaps you should switch to water?"

"Perhaps you should mind your business." Li said with a wink. "Now, more Tang please."

Igor plucked a packet of Tang from the food supply bin. Li noticed a twinkle in Igor's eye. Igor loved playing tricks, and Li sensed he was up to something.

"No tricks, Igor! Just give me the Tang!"

"As you wish," Igor giggled.

Igor ripped open the juice bag and squeezed. In a world without gravity, the juice spurted toward Li in great orange globs.

"Hey!" Li shouted.

Igor laughed. "Drink up my friend! Ha Ha Ha!"

"Commander Steal!" Li whined, rubbing the juice from his face.

"Easy boys," Commander Patti Steal said with authority. She looked sternly at the Tang floating all around her. "How did juice get everywhere?"

"He started it!" Igor and Li said at once. Commander Patti Steal shook her head. "I'm sorry I asked. No more horsing around."

"Yes, Commander," the other astronauts said. Patti Steal ran a tight spaceship. They did not want to cross her. She peered at one of the computers. She frowned when she noticed a red warning light.

"What's wrong?" Li asked.

"Our communication light is flashing red. We've lost contact with Earth." Commander Steal said.

Igor gasped. "That's bad news, what do we do?"

Losing contact with Earth put them in serious danger. The communication link had to be fixed—fast.

Patti Steal floated to her command center. Computers lined every wall. A small porthole gazed out into space. In the distance, Earth glowed like a beautiful blue marble.

She sat in her command chair and gave her orders. "Li, I think you've had enough Tang. Go check the communication log and find out how we lost contact. Igor, suit up; I want you to inspect the transmitters for damage."

"Aye, Commander," Igor and Li said together. They liked to play around, but they were serious astronauts when it was time to work.

Meanwhile, Commander Patti Steal tried to make contact with Earth.

"Houston, this is Commander Patti Steal at the International Space Station. Do you read me? Houston, do you copy my transmission?"

A crackle of static was the only response.

Yung Li looked up from his computer. "Commander, we lost contact exactly four minutes ago. My calculations show that a massive burst of energy knocked out our transmitter."

Commander Steal was shocked. "Something fishy is going on here..." she said. "Igor, I want that transmitter repaired ASAP."

"Aye Commander!" Igor said. He had just finished putting on his space suit. "I'm ready to work. Permission to exit the Space Station?"

Commander Patti Steal nodded. "Permission granted. I'm sending you into space now."

"Roger." Igor said.

She pushed the **JETTISON** button.

The doorway to space opened. Silver light from a trillion twinkling stars glowed against Igor's face. Two quick bursts from Igor's jet pack pushed him up and out into space.

"Commander Steal," Igor said over the radio. "I see our transmitters. They're all smashed up!"

"Do you think you can fix it?" Commander Steal asked.

"I don't know... let me see what I can do!"

Igor uncoiled a tether from his gear belt and strapped himself to the hull so he could work without floating away. Earth glowed peacefully in the distance.

But the peace did not last.

A warning signal beeped on Yung Li's computer.

"What's wrong?" Commander Steal asked.

Li shook his head. "Something big is approaching us, but I can't see it!"

"Try to lock it down," Commander Steal said. She spoke into her radio. "Igor, what's the situation outside?"

"There is a lot of damage, but I think I can fix it ... h-hey wait a minute... something is out here..."

There was a long pause.

At once all the light from the sun and the stars vanished. A huge black shadow draped the ISS in darkness. Yung Li's computer short-circuited. "I'm losing control of my systems!" he shouted. Sparks flew against his face.

Emergency alarms wailed.

Patti Steal yelled into her radio. "Igor! What's going on out there?!"

"It's so hideous! It's so horrible! Oh noooo!!"

A mighty *BOOM* shook the Space Station. A swarm of metallic wings flapped outside.

"Bats?!" Commander Steal gasped. It was impossible. It couldn't be. There were no bats in space!

Something big landed on the Space Station. With heavy thuds it prowled along the hull. It seized Igor with its robotic claw, taking him prisoner. A deep, evil laugh thundered outside.

"MUAH! HA! HA!"

Chapter 2: Executive Decision

One Hour Later, The White House, Washington D.C.

News of the attack at the ISS spread at light speed. Outside the White House, the presidential helicopter landed just moments after dawn.

President Hamm waved to the crowd of news cameras. At the steps of the White House, a group of generals and scientists eagerly awaited him. The news reporters wasted no time bombarding him with questions.

"Was the ISS destroyed?"

"Did aliens kidnap our astronauts?"

"Who is to blame for this mess?"

A stern voice boomed across the lawn. "There will be no comments for the press at this time."

It was General Guerra. He was the President's top military advisor. General Guerra had a strong chin and a broad chest covered in shiny medals.

"We need answers!" A reporter shouted.

"Not until we figure out what is going on up there," General Guerra said.

More flashing cameras. More questions.

President Hamm and General Guerra walked up the White House steps. "We can't stall them forever," the President said. "The press has to know what happened. Do we have any information?"

"It's bad," the General said. "Real bad." They walked into the Oval Office and closed the door.

"Give it to me straight," the President said. "What happened to the astronauts?"

"Mr. President, this may be the single greatest threat to our national security in history."

General Guerra pulled a projector screen from the ceiling and dimmed the lights. An image of the International Space Station glowed on the screen.

"Here is what we know: about an hour ago, NASA lost contact with the ISS. Commander Patti Steal sent a distress signal, but something cut it off."

"Distress signal?" the President gasped. "What happened?"

"One of our satellites captured a brief video of what happened." General Guerra then became very serious. "Mr. President, I have to warn you, what you are about to see is very disturbing. You should sit down."

"I will not sit while brave astronaut's *lives* are at stake! Show me what happened!"

"As you wish." General Guerra said. A fuzzy image flashed across the screen.

"What the devil?" President Hamm muttered. A tall dark figure loomed over the Space Station. Dozens of metallic things swarmed around it.

President Hamm peered at the figure. When he realized who it was, his knees went wobbly. With effort he found his seat and took a breath. "In all my years as President, I never thought I would see *him* again."

"We still don't know how he escaped the maximum-security prison on Mars. But one thing is for sure; Doctor NoseBleed is back, and he's more powerful than ever."

"Well let's not waste time! Send a rescue team right away!"

General Guerra nodded. "I already alerted the Space Marines. They have orders rescue the astronauts and place Doctor NoseBleed under arrest. It will be dangerous, but they must succeed. I have only one request."

"Anything."

"It's no accident that Doctor NoseBleed hijacked the ISS. I think he's planning something... something very, very evil. I want our top guy on this."

President Hamm knew who that was. The US Government's top agent was in high demand these days.

General Guerra continued, "He's the only person that has ever defeated Doctor NoseBleed in battle. I don't want to do anything until we get him here in Washington."

"I just sent him on a very important mission not long ago. He's a very busy boy..."

"You know the stakes, Mr. President. We need him."

President Hamm nodded. "Very well, I'll arrange a ride." He leaned forward and picked up a bright red phone. "This is the President. I need a helicopter sent to Evergreen Elementary School right away. Tell the pilot his passenger is very important. The passenger must be brought to the White House immediately. It is a matter of *national security!*"

"Yes sir!" the voice on the other end of the line said. "Who is the passenger?"

President Hamm gazed out his window. Somewhere out there, three brave astronauts were in terrible danger. Their best hope for survival rested on one boy's shoulders.

"*Snot Rocket.*"

Chapter 3: Ahh Choo!

Evergreen Elementary School

Fourth grade was hard at Evergreen Elementary, especially for the kids in Miz Rubble's class.

Miz Rubble had no patience for children who misbehaved. She even trained her grumpy old cat to patrol the classroom like a prison guard. Together they constantly searched for troublemakers.

Late to school? Detention!

Forget your homework? Detention!

Giggling in class? You guessed it. *Detention!*

Miz Rubble's sharp eyes fell on the single empty desk in class. "Well... well..." she said. "Where is Mr. Rocket today?"

Snot Rocket was tardy more than any other student, and his excuses were always too strange to be true. She glanced suspiciously at Harry Pitts.

"You're his best friend, right Mr. Pitts?" She said with an accusing tone.

"Y-yes Miz Rubble!" poor Harry Pitts squeaked. He was always a well-behaved boy. He was also the best math-wiz in school. But Miz Rubble knew that Harry Pitts and Snot Rocket were friends. She leaned close to get a confession.

"Then tell me… Where is Mr. Rocket? He had better not come in here late again with one of his high-flying excuses!"

Harry shrunk beneath her glare. Right on cue, the classroom door flew wide open.

Snot Rocket burst into the classroom. To everyone's surprise, he was soaking wet!

"I'm here! I'm here!" he yelled. He held his completed homework high over his head. "I came as fast as I could!"

Snot shook the water from his hair and face. He dropped all his finished homework onto Miz Rubble's desk.

Snot was about the same height as the other kids. But he really stood out in a crowd. Snot had *the largest* nose in school. In fact, he had the largest nose in the whole state!

Snot had a genetic mutation. Scientists called it a *Nuclear Nostril,* and it was very rare and powerful. If you knew one thing about Snot's Nuclear Nostril, it was this; you did *not* want to be too close when he sneezed!

A puddle of salty ocean water pooled around Snot's shoes. A little fish flipped out of his pocket and flopped on the floor. Miz Rubble's grumpy old cat meowed hungrily and licked its fangs as it watched the little fish.

"My goodness!" Miz Rubble said. "Late again! And why are you all wet?"

"It's a long story," Snot said. He walked over to his desk and took a seat. "It all started with an earthquake..."

Miz Rubble raised a thin eyebrow. "An earthquake you say?"

"Yes Ma'am. There was a huge earthquake off the coast of Australia. It sent tremors thousands of miles across the ocean until they formed a giant wave called a tsunami!"

No one believed Snot's story—except for Harry Pitts of course. Harry always believed in his friend.

"So..." Miz Rubble said. "An earthquake near Australia caused tsunami? I still see no excuse for being late."

"Well that's not all!" Snot said defensively. "A ship was right in the tsunami's path, so I had to—

"That is enough!" Miz Rubble interrupted.

"I've had it! Earthquakes and tsunamis and all this nonsense... you'll be serving detention after school!"

"But..."

"Beg your pardon?" Miz Rubble fumed. "Double Detention! And that better be the last I hear of this silly story."

Snot dipped his head sadly. "Yes Ma'am."

Miz Rubble huffed. Her grumpy old cat scowled.

"Now, back to today's work," she said.

She turned to write on the chalkboard. In big white letters she wrote the words *Science Fair*.

"All of you will submit a full presentation. We are studying outer space and the galaxies. I expect only top-notch work!" She glanced back at Snot. "And *no* projects will be accepted late, am I understood?"

"Yes, Miz Rubble," the class said together.

Miz Rubble then scribbled some math problems on the chalk board. Meanwhile, the silver fish wriggled in a puddle by Snot's desk.

Miz Rubble's cat purred hungrily. The cat jumped onto Snot's desk to get closer to the tasty fish.

"No cat, go away!" Snot whispered.

A silver fin flashed. In an instant the cat jumped down to catch it.

What happened next was a disaster.

When the cat jumped, its furry tail flipped up and tickled the tip of Snot's nose. Snot sniffled at first, then he snorted. "Oh no!" he gasped.

Snot's big nose scrunched up. "Ahh..."

"Miz Rubble! Snot's gonna sneeze!" one of the kids shouted.

Miz Rubble panicked. She dropped her chalk and dove behind her desk. "Everyone take cover!"

All the kids screamed and jumped beneath their desks. Snot felt his Nuclear Nostril tingling. There was no stopping it now.

"AHHHH *CHOOOOO!!!!!*"

A tremendous blast erupted from Snot's nose with the force of a tornado.

Snot's sneeze blasted a huge crater through the wall of Miz Rubble's classroom. Desks were thrown clear across the school. Backpacks and lunchboxes and anything else not bolted down was blown away.

When the dust settled, Harry Pitts poked his head out from under his charred desk. He looked up at Snot and gave him an awkward smile.

"Bless you!"

Chapter 4: Triple Detention

Snot was in BIG trouble.

His massive sneeze reduced Miz Rubble's classroom to rubble. One by one, the students poked their heads out from under their desks. No one was hurt, but there were more than a few singed hairs.

Miz Rubble wiped the debris from her glasses.

"Mister Rocket!!" She fumed.

Her old grumpy cat was clinging to the ceiling and meowing angrily. The tip of his tail was burned completely off! Snot winced it his seat. He really did it this time.

"Triple Detention!" Miz Rubble declared. "Get yourself to Principal Bard's office this instant! To the Stool of Shame with you!"

"Oh no, not the Stool of Shame..." Snot groaned. Snot slumped his shoulders and looked at his classmates. "Sorry everyone, I didn't mean to blow up the class, honest."

"I said *out!*" Miz Rubble yelled.

Snot climbed out from the smoky ruins of the classroom. Seconds later, Principal Bard burst into the hallway. He waved his arms in a panic.

"Tornado! We're doomed!" He screamed. Then he saw Snot standing in the hall. Embarrassed, Principal Bard quickly regained his composure. "Oh... I thought we were trapped in a cyclone. I guess you sneezed again, didn't you?"

"It was an accident, I swear!" Snot said.

"Accident or not, that is destruction of school property." Principal Bard said. He loomed over Snot like a tower. "Go sit on the Stool of Shame and think about what you've done."

Snot sat in silence. Looking out the open window, he wished his sneezes weren't so powerful.

Moments later, deep thumping sounds rattled the windows. A shadow passed over the school. Above the playground, flags whipped wildly in the wind.

A gust of air blew Principal Bard's papers everywhere. "What is going on now!?" He shouted. His eyes nearly jumped from his head when he saw what was causing all the commotion.

A black helicopter hovered right over the school. "What is the meaning of this?" Principal Bard gasped.

From the helicopter, a man in black tactical gear tossed a rope over the side and rappelled down to the school.

The agent had dark sunglasses and a blonde mustache. With a powerful voice he boomed "My name is Agent Dare, I'm from the CIA." He flashed a badge. "My orders come directly from the President of the United States. Where is Snot Rocket?"

Miz Rubble ran down the hall to see what was happening. She turned pale when she saw the hovering chopper and the powerful-looking CIA agent. Agent Dare spotted the young boy on the Stool of Shame. "Mr. Rocket, I have orders to take you to the White House."

Snot looked up at Agent Dare. "I'd love to, but I have triple detention."

"Triple detention?" Agent Dare asked.

"Yeah. I'm not allowed to leave the Stool of Shame." Snot answered.

"It's a matter of urgent national security," Agent Dare said. "I have my orders."

Miz Rubble intervened. "He has been very naughty! He is not to leave the Stool of Shame!"

Agent Dare shrugged. "Well, since you can't leave the Stool of Shame, we'll just have to take it with us. Come along, Mr. Rocket, the President needs you now more than ever."

Agent Dare strapped a utility belt around Snot's waist. With a *whoosh* Agent Dare and Snot Rocket were whisked up to the hovering helicopter.

"Welcome aboard, Mr. Rocket," the helicopter pilot said. "I'm Captain Hawk, I'll be taking you to the White House."

"Captain Hawk is the best pilot in the CIA." Agent Dare added. "He can fly anything."

"Pleased to meet you." Snot said. Then, over the sound of the rotors, a shrill voiced made everyone wince.

"I still expect your homework to be completed on time!" Miz Rubble shouted. "This is no excuse!"

"*Sheesh*, what's her problem?" Captain Hawk asked.

"She's Miz Rubble." Snot answered.

Captain Hawk chuckled. "You can say that again."

Chapter 5: The Weapon of Math Destruction

Meanwhile, at the ISS

"Muah Ha Ha!"

Doctor NoseBleed's menacing laugh echoed across the Space Station. He was hard at work modifying the computers. Within a few short hours, he completely rebuilt the ISS to suit his evil plan.

Magnetic boots kept him firmly planted on the floor. Meanwhile, his prisoners floated helplessly in zero gravity. Astronauts Igor Popov, Yung Li, and Commander Patti Steal were lashed together like a bundle of logs. They floated past the main window that faced Earth.

The beautiful blue marble was obscured by a wretched swarm of black wings.

"What are those things?" Igor whispered to the others. "There are *hundreds* of them!"

"They look like bats." Yung Li observed.

"They look like robots to me." Patti Steal said.

"Whatever they are, they're *hideous*!" Igor said.

Doctor NoseBleed turned to face them. His powerful cyborg eye glowed like a hot coal. "Ah... I see you are admiring my loyal army of RoBATs! They are robotic bats from space! They will guard the ISS during the final phase of my brilliant plan."

"You'll never get away with this, NoseBleed!" Commander Patti Steal said defiantly.

"That's *Doctor* NoseBleed to you, Commander. And yes, I *will* get away with it."

Doctor NoseBleed tossed back his scarlet cape, revealing his mechanical arm. The astronauts gasped. It was equipped with a cruel-looking claw that sent a chill down their human spines. Doctor NoseBleed pointed out the main window.

"Behold! My most glorious invention yet!"

Outside, several RoBATs were moving a massive laser into position. Doctor NoseBleed pulled a transmitter from his coat pocket to give his orders.

"Mount it on top of the Space Station," he said. "We will test the laser in *five minutes*!"

The RoBATs' antennas flashed red to signal their obedience. They were machines—nothing more.

Their unthinking, unfeeling computer-brains did their master's bidding with cold precision.

Doctor NoseBleed activated several computer screens. Each showed a video feed from a different location on Earth. One of the screens displayed a single black helicopter flying high over a forest.

"What are you planning, Doctor NoseBleed?" Patti Steal asked angrily.

"I will answer your question with another question, Commander. Tell me, what do you think would happen if one day . . . math disappeared?"

It was a bizarre question. An impossible question. No math? How could it be? Patti Steal shook her head. "That could never happen. Math is everywhere, we use it every day. No math? That's impossible."

"Oh, it's possible. Tell me what you think would happen if math was simply . . . *destroyed?*"

Commander Steal cringed at the thought. "It would be terrible. Anything that uses math would stop working. Phones, electrical grids, the Internet ... it would all fall apart! Doctors wouldn't know how much medicine to give a sick patient. Money wouldn't work, because no one would be able to count or make change. Civilization would collapse. If math were destroyed, it would send humanity back to the Stone Age! A world without math would be horrible."

"Yes, very horrible." Doctor NoseBleed said. "So horrible, that people would to do *anything* to keep it from happening. Once the world's leaders witness my awesome power, they will have no choice but to surrender. Then they will hail *me* as their Global Overlord. Muah Ha Ha!"

"He's a madman!" Yung Li gasped.

"It doesn't matter what would happen *if* you could destroy math." Patti Steal said sharply. "It's impossible! You're just a crazy cyborg with a broken microchip for a brain."

"Crazy?" Doctor NoseBleed said angrily. "You think I am crazy? Ha! You know nothing. Perhaps a demonstration is necessary."

He traced a finger along the wall of screens. "Hmm . . ." he thought out loud. He saw the video of the helicopter flying over the forest. He stopped.

"What is he doing?" Igor whispered.

Doctor NoseBleed watched the helicopter. It was deep in the wilderness, far from any witnesses. It was a perfect test-target. "Yes . . . yes that will do nicely!" Doctor NoseBleed said.

He pushed a button on his transmitter. "RoBATs! Prepare to fire the WMD!"

"WMD?" The astronauts asked at once.

Doctor NoseBleed flashed a wicked grin.

"Yes... Weapon of *MATH* Destruction!"

Chapter 6: Crash Landing

Inside the helicopter, Agent Dare pulled out a tablet computer. He swiped through the plans for the rescue mission. Outside the helicopter windows, tall mountains and green forests blurred by.

Agent Dare zoomed in on a picture of the disaster unfolding on the ISS. He held it up for Snot Rocket to see.

"It's Doctor NoseBleed. We're sure of it." Agent Dare explained.

"I'm not afraid of NoseBleed, but we shouldn't underestimate that sneaky cyborg. What's the plan?"

"As we speak, the Space Marines preparing to launch." Agent Dare said.

28

"Space Marines?" Snot asked.

Agent Dare nodded. "They're specially trained for dangerous missions in space. Only the best and brightest can lead the Space Marines, and the President picked *you* for the job. Together, we will rescue the astronauts bring Doctor NoseBleed to justice."

"I beat him once, I can do it again." Snot Rocket said confidently.

Agent Dare grinned. "Excellent! President Hamm ordered NASA to prepare a shuttle to take us into space." He showed Snot the charts and equations on the computer screen. "Here is the flight plan for the rocket. It will be a dangerous mission," he warned. "The Space Marines are tough, but they can't defeat Doctor NoseBleed without you."

Snot nodded. "You can count on me . . . Hey, what's that?"

A green light flashed in the sky. It was so bright that Agent Dare, Captain Hawk, and Snot Rocket all had to shield their eyes.

Suddenly, things started to go very wrong.

First, the computer screen in Agent Dare's hand flickered. All the math and equations on the screen swirled like crazy. The numbers transformed into complete gibberish!

Things got worse.

The helicopter's engine sputtered, stuttered and shuddered. Then it spun out of control!

"What's happening?" Agent Dare shouted.

"I can't measure fuel or thrust!" Captain Hawk cried. "The math in my control panel has stopped working!"

"How can that be?" Agent Dare gasped. The helicopter plummeted down to the earth. Without math or functioning controls, Captain Hawk was powerless to stop them from falling. Snot looked out the window; everything was spinning around them!

"Prepare for impact!" Captain Hawk yelled. An emergency alarm buzzed.

Snot had to do something to save their lives—fast! There wasn't much time, but he had an idea.

"Everyone hang on!" Snot shouted. "I'll only get one shot at this!"

There was no time for questions. Agent Dare and Captain Hawk braced themselves.

Snot crawled to the helicopter's door and swung it open. Wind blew against him so hard that he had to hold on tight to keep from falling. The ground below was approaching fast. *I sure hope this works!*

He pinched his nose and built up pressure in his Nuclear Nostril.

"What's he doing?" Captain Hawk shouted.

"His Nuclear Nostril has many different powers." Agent Dare answered over the howling wind. "It won't be pretty, but I think Snot can save us!"

Won't be pretty? Captain Hawk wondered. *What does that mean?*

Snot Rocket felt the power in his nose grew hotter and stronger.

"It's too late! We're going to crash!" Captain Hawk screamed. He and Agent Dare clenched their eyes shut. *This it, we're toast!* They both thought.

There was an ear-splitting *BOOM!* And the helicopter seemed to shake more violently than ever. But it wasn't from a crash.

Something hot and goopy splashed all over Agent Dare and Captain Hawk. Then, as if by magic, the free-falling helicopter stopped in midair. Like a butterfly it floated up for a moment, then hit the ground with a soft *thud!*

Agent Dare was the first to open his eyes. "We aren't dead!"

"It's a miracle!" Captain Hawk cheered.

Then both of their faces scrunched up.

Green gooey slime covered the entire helicopter. It dripped from the ceiling. It oozed from the sides. It bubbled up from the floor.

"Gross!" they both gasped.

Snot wiped the goo from his nose. "I had to act fast, sorry about the mess guys."

Agent Dare swatted slime from his mustache. He reached out and shook Snot's hand. "If you ask me, I'd rather get blasted with slime than die in a helicopter crash."

Captain Hawk wiped goo from his face. "I agree! How did you know to do that?"

"Simple physics." Snot answered matter-of-factly. "An object in motion will remain in motion, until an equal or greater force stops it. I waited until we were just a few feet above the ground. When the time was right, I released just enough power from my Nuclear Nostril to stop us in midair. Then gravity brought us back to the ground."

"Genius," Captain Hawk said with a smile. "I can see why the President trusts you."

Agent Dare held some of the goo between his thumb and forefinger. He looked at it closely. "Wait a minute. What is all this goo anyway?" he asked. "Please tell me it's not what I think it is."

"Oh no..." Captain Hawk groaned. "Don't tell me it's ..."

Snot shrugged. "Well, they don't call me _Snot_ Rocket for nothing."

Chapter 7: Destroy Snot Rocket!

Back at the ISS

Doctor NoseBleed was pleased. His WMD performed even better than expected. Seconds after the laser hit the helicopter, the aircraft spun like a top and fell from the sky.

"Without math, nothing will be able to fly!" Doctor NoseBleed declared. "Look! The helicopter is out of control. Muah Ha Ha!"

An explosion lit up the screen. The helicopter disappeared behind a wall of smoke and fire. The astronauts gasped in horror.

"You maniac!" Patti Steal snarled. "Innocent people were on that helicopter! You're a murderer!"

Doctor NoseBleed glared at her. His evil cyborg eye glowed red with fury. "I grow tired of your heroics, Commander. One more peep and I'll jettison you into space!"

It was a deadly threat. There is no oxygen in space, and the temperatures are far below zero. Commander Steal would freeze and suffocate all at once. But Doctor NoseBleed didn't scare her.

"Peep!" she shouted defiantly.

"You will pay for your insolence!" Doctor NoseBleed roared. He lunged at her with his mechanical arm.

An alarm buzzed. The noise was so sudden that it stopped Doctor NoseBleed in his tracks. Warning lights flashed. Doctor NoseBleed left Patti Steal alone and hurried to see what was happening. He stared at the computer screen in disbelief. "What? How is that possible?"

Doctor NoseBleed watched as the smoke from the helicopter crash floated away. The helicopter was damaged, but somehow, it wasn't destroyed. How could that be? He'd seen the explosion! If all that smoke and fire didn't come from a crash, where *did* it come from?

Bright green goo surrounded the helicopter. Goo like that only came from one place. A shiver went down Doctor NoseBleed's spine.

"I've seen that green goo before..." he stuttered. "Zoom in on that video!"

The computer obeyed and zoomed in on the helicopter crash. A CIA agent with a gold mustache climbed out of the wreck. He then reached down to help someone out of the helicopter. A boy with a huge nose emerged from the crash and hopped on the ground. Doctor NoseBleed slammed his fist into a wall.

"*Snot Rocket!*" he wailed. "My worst enemy!"

Patti Steal smirked at him. "Looks like your goose is cooked! Give up now and maybe Snot Rocket will go easy on you."

Doctor NoseBleed quickly regained his composure. "Don't get your hopes up, Commander. No one will be able to save you now, not even Snot Rocket!"

Doctor NoseBleed could see that Snot Rocket was vulnerable. He saw an opportunity to score an easy victory. His cyborg-brain formed an evil plan of attack.

"I'll rid myself of that meddling do-gooder once and for all..." Doctor NoseBleed said. He pulled out his transmitter. "RoBATs! Go down to Earth and *destroy Snot Rocket!*"

"*No!*" Patti Steal yelled. Outside the Space Station, hundreds of robotic wings flapped as the RoBATs flew down to Earth.

"Now, Snot Rocket will meet his doom!" Doctor NoseBleed laughed. He pressed button. At once all the computer screens showed a live video of Snot Rocket down on Earth. "In a few minutes, my swarm of RoBATs will tear Snot Rocket apart." He glanced at the astronauts and grinned. "Prepare to witness your hero's demise! Muah Ha Ha!"

Patti Steal looked to the other astronauts. "We have to escape," she whispered, "or else this maniac is going to destroy the world!"

"But how can we stop him?" Li said.

Commander Patti Steal winked. "It's risky, but think I have a plan..."

Chapter 8: A Sticky Situation

Deep in the woods, location unknown.

Green goo from Snot's Nuclear Nostril was everywhere. Smoke billowed from the damaged helicopter. Snot Rocket, Agent Dare, and Captain Hawk helped each other out of the wreck one at a time. Captain Hawk looked at the damage and let out a low whistle. "*Whew*, I'm afraid this helicopter is in bad shape," he said.

"Can you fix it?" Agent Dare asked. The pilot shook his head.

"Not without a new set of rotors. They got completely sheared off during the crash."

"Blast!" Agent Dare said. "Can you call for help?"

"The radio is covered in goo, but if I clean it up I might be able to send a signal to Washington."

Agent Dare nodded. "Do what you can. In the meantime, I'll try to figure out where we landed. Hopefully there's a road or something nearby."

"I'll help." Snot offered.

Together, Snot Rocket and Agent Dare explored the area. After a few minutes of searching, Snot tugged on Agent Dare's arm. He pointed to a metal sign bolted against a fence.

Snot read the sign. "It says 'X–Machina.' What's an X–Machina?"

Agent Dare's jaw dropped. "My goodness. I can't believe we're here!"

"What do you mean?" Snot asked.

"X–Machina is a top-secret government lab," Agent Dare explained. "Its purpose is to study extraterrestrial lifeforms."

"*Aliens?*" Snot asked. "Do you really think there might be aliens here?"

Agent Dare nodded. "If the X–Machina is close, then we need to be extra cautious," he said. He looked around. He watched the trees suspiciously, as if he thought they were being watched.

"Is X-Machina dangerous?" Snot asked quietly.

"I don't know." Agent Dare answered. "But be ready for anything. There's no telling what strange creatures we may encounter at the X–Machina base."

"Ok." Snot said. "We should probably warn Captain Hawk."

"Agreed," Agent Dare said.

Suddenly, a hair-raising scream erupted behind them. "Help! Help! They're everywhere!"

Snot and Agent Dare looked at each other. "Captain Hawk!" they exclaimed together. Without hesitation, they ran toward Captain Hawk's cries for help.

Chapter 9: Attack of the RoBATs

Awful metallic screeches filled the air. "Bats!!" Agent Dare shouted. Over their heads, hundreds of horrible black creatures swarmed. They blotted out the sun like an evil cloud.

One of the RoBATs spotted Snot Rocket. It's wicked computer-brain locked onto him and prepared to attack. Like a dive-bomber, it tucked its wings and swooped in for the kill. "Snot watch out!" Agent Dare yelled.

Snot jumped behind a tree for cover and the RoBAT slammed into the trunk with a *THWACK!*

"Nice moves!" Agent Dare said. "But it might not be enough, look!"

He pointed to the helicopter. Nearly a dozen RoBATs had picked up Captain Hawk. They started to fly away with him trapped in their claws. His arms and legs flailed wildly. "Help me, Snot!" he screamed.

Snot pointed his nose at the swarm of RoBATs. "You might want to stand back," he said to Agent Dare. Snot knew that only his special Booger Blaster attack could save Captain Hawk now. Snot pressed a thumb against his nose and warmed up his Nuclear Nostril. "Bombs away!" Snot called out.

Boom! Boom! Boom! Boom!

Snot fired off a volley of explosive boogers from his nuclear nostril. Black puffs of smoke burst all around the pilot as Snot Rocket blasted RoBATs clear out of the sky.

"Yeah! Let 'em have it!" Agent Dare cheered.

Two RoBATs, three RoBATs, *four* RoBATs exploded in the air. Nuts and bolts and broken wings fell to the ground. In an instant Captain Hawk was released from their grip.

"Ahhhhh!!!" Captain Hawk screamed as he fell. Snot hurried to save him. Snot aimed his nose downward and fired his last Booger Blaster downward. The blast launched his body into the sky like a missile.

"Incoming!" Snot yelled. He summersaulted toward Captain Hawk and caught him in midair. "Now hold on, this is gonna be a rough landing!"

They fell a full hundred feet toward the ground. Seconds before impact, Snot blew a burst of power from his nose to slow down their fall, just like he did on the helicopter. Snot Rocket and Captain Hawk landed on the grass with a gentle thud. They were safe for the moment, but Snot's heroic defense failed to take out all the RoBATs. Dozens more were still in the sky—waiting for the right moment to strike.

Captain Hawk didn't realize that they were still in grave danger. "Wow! That's *two* I owe you, Snot!" he said with a smile. "Thanks!"

"Don't thank me just yet." Snot said. He had a worried look on his face.

"What's wrong?" Agent Dare asked.

Snot tapped his nose. "I'm out of Booger Blasters!"

"Out of Booger Blasters?" Captain Hawk asked, worried.

Snot nodded grimly. "I can only blast so many boogers before my Nuclear Nostril needs to recharge," he explained.

"How long does that take?" Agent Dare asked.

Snot looked up. Above them, the RoBATs circled like vultures.

Snot gulped. "Too long," he said. "Looks like we are in for some hand-to-wing combat, guys."

The RoBATs swooped down.

"Here they come!" Snot yelled.

Chapter 10: Doctor NoseBleed Victorious

Meanwhile, up in space...

"Muah Ha Ha!" Doctor NoseBleed laughed.

Every computer screen in the Space Station displayed the battle on Earth in high definition. After several minutes of fighting, many RoBATs lay in pieces around Snot Rocket and his friends. Snot had put up a better fight than Doctor NoseBleed expected, but his efforts were futile.

Eventually, Snot's Nuclear Nostril ran out of boogers to blast, just as Doctor NoseBleed knew he would.

Doctor NoseBleed snickered.

"Looks like Snot Rocket is all out of Booger Blasters. Now he is truly defenseless!"

"Let him go, NoseBleed!" Commander Patti Steal said. "You have your victory, don't hurt him!"

"Hurt him? No Commander, I am not going to *hurt* him..."

He pressed a button on his transmitter.

"RoBATs! After you _kill_ Snot Rocket, I want you to *bring me his nose!*"

The astronauts gasped in horror. Snot Rocket was surrounded by dozens of powerful RoBATs. If the astronauts didn't do something to help, then Snot Rocket would be defeated.

Doctor NoseBleed turned on his heels and typed wildly on a nearby keyboard. Outside the Space Station, eerie green lights flashed as the WMD warmed up. "With Snot Rocket out of the way, I can now unleash the true power of my Weapon of Math Destruction. My first target? The Internet! Muah Ha Ha!"

A green laser blasted from the WMD and collided with Earth. In an instant, computers all over the planet went haywire. Without math, the Internet couldn't work. Billions of people stared at blank screens in terror. The Internet was just *gone.* Doctor NoseBleed laughed harder than ever.

"Ahaha! Victory is mine!"

Yung Li looked at his fellow astronauts. "Commander Steal," Li whispered, "if you still have a plan to get us out of here, I think we'd better try it!"

Commander Steal nodded. "I agree. We have to take a chance. Do we have anymore Tang?"

"More Tang?" Igor asked, puzzled. Yung Li grinned when he realized what she was planning.

"I keep a secret stash behind my computer. I just really love Tang."

The astronauts' arms were tightly bound, but their legs were still free. As the Space Station orbited the Earth, they bounced against the walls like a pin-ball. When Commander Steal saw that they were about to hit a wall again. She put her plan into action.

"On my signal, I want everyone to kick that wall with all their strength." she whispered. "We'll aim for Li's computer station. Then Li will release all the Tang he has!"

"Aye-aye, Commander." Yung Li whispered.

Igor nudged the others. "We're floating toward the wall now."

Commander Patti Steal started the countdown. "Three... Two... One! Everyone kick!"

The astronauts bounced against the wall. Instead of gently floating away, they all kicked hard and rocketed across the Space Station. It happened so fast that Doctor NoseBleed missed when he tried to snatch them with his robotic claw.

Doctor NoseBleed chased after them. "Escape is impossible!" he roared. "I'll catch you soon enough!"

"Catch this!" Patti Steal yelled. Right on cue, Yung Li smashed open his secret compartment with his boot. Glass shattered and a huge wave orange-flavored Tang spilled out of the broken compartment.

Big globs of Tang splattered against Doctor NoseBleed's face. The juice got into his cyborg eye and caused it to short-circuit.

"Aaarrrghhh!!!" Doctor NoseBleed bellowed. Sparks slew from his damaged eye. He and fell into a wall filled with control panels—smashing them to pieces. Suddenly, the Weapon of Math Destruction swiveled uncontrollably outside.

"No!" Doctor NoseBleed screamed. "The targeting system! It's been destroyed!"

Now the WMD was more dangerous than ever. Green lasers collided with Earth at random. Each time, the WMD destroyed math in some unlucky corner of the globe.

A computerized voice echoed across the station.

"Warning! Warning! The X-Machina base has been hit! Repeat: The X-Machina base has been hit!"

"No!" Doctor NoseBleed cried. "You fools! Do you know what you have done?!"

The astronauts gulped. Their plan to help Snot Rocket had backfired—*badly*.

"The X-Machina base holds some of the most dangerous aliens in the galaxy!" he said.

"The locks use complex math equations to keep the aliens from escaping. A direct hit from my WMD could unleash them!"

"How do you know all this?" Commander Patti Steal asked.

"The prison on Mars has the same kind of locks. I invented the WMD to escape from my cell!" He typed furiously on his keyboard. He hacked into the X-Machina computer system. Bright red letters flashed across his computer screen.

X-Machina Prisoner Report ...

Checking Files ...

WARNING! WARNING!

Lock Failure in Cell Block 1!

"Oh no..." NoseBleed stuttered. "One of the X-Machina locks was hit! You've doomed us all!"

WARNING! WARNING!

Alien Activity in Cell Block 1!

WARNING! WARNING!

Dangerous Alien Identified!

Space Lifeform from Uranus: Gastropod - Gets Extremely Radioactive (SLUGGER)

STATUS: PRISONER ESCAPED!

Chapter 11: Space Lifeform from Uranus: Gastropod – Gets Extremely Radioactive (SLUGGER)

Back on Earth, Near the X-Machina Base

Things were going very badly for Snot Rocket.

RoBATs surrounded him on all sides. "We have to fight our way out!" Snot said to his friends.

"There are too many of them!" Captain Hawk yelled. Black wings swarmed. Screeching, biting, scratching RoBATs hammered at the humans without mercy. Snot punched a RoBAT right in the face. He knocked it out, but two more took its place. Meanwhile, Agent Dare leaned back and karate-kicked a RoBAT so hard that it's wings snapped off.

"Behind you!" Snot yelled. But it was too late. A RoBAT swooped down tackled Agent Dare to the ground. "Run Snot! Run while you still can!" Agent Dare yelled.

"I won't leave you behind!" Snot said. He tried to help Agent Dare back to his feet, but a RoBAT grabbed Snot's arm. Then another latched onto his leg. Soon, Snot had a RoBAT tugging on all four of his limbs.

He struggled to break free, but there were too many RoBATs for him to fight on his own.

Right when all hope seemed lost, a distant rumble caught Captain Hawk's attention.

"What is that?!" Captain Hawk yelled.

Somewhere in the mountains, an alarm from the secret X-Machina base blared. It was so loud that it even startled the RoBATs. A computerized voice echoed from the base.

"Emergency! Emergency! Prisoner Escaped!"

"Oh no." Agent Dare said over the alarms. "An alien must have escaped from the base!"

"As if things could get any worse?" Captain Hawk yelled, swatting at RoBATs as he did.

"I think they're about to!" Snot replied.

Brilliant purple light erupted from the side of the mountain. Seconds later something hurled toward them like a cannon-ball. The round object whistled high overhead and arced downward.

"Everyone duck!" Snot yelled.

The mysterious round thing slammed into the army of RoBATs. It hit the RoBATs so hard that they scattered everywhere like bowling pins.

Before Snot could get a good look, the round thing bounced up from the pile of destroyed RoBATs and rolled into a thicket of bushes.

"Gadzooks! What on Earth was that??" Captain Hawk said. Agent Dare looked nervously at the bushes where the mysterious flying object landed.

"I don't think it's anything from Earth..." he said. "Snot, get ready to fight!"

Snot shook his head. "Whatever that was, it just destroyed all the RoBATs. I think it's on *our* side."

Agent Dare said, "It still might be dangerous—

Loud rustling cut off his words. Eerie light glowed from behind the bushes. "Here it comes!" Captain Hawk said.

Two long eyes popped up. Bright purple skin glistened under the sun.

"Is that a snail?" Snot asked.

"It's huge!" Captain Hawk gasped.

The creature emerged from the bushes and revealed itself. A faint glow of blue light glowed around it. It was the biggest and most colorful snail any of them had ever seen. Even more bizarre, it had a titanium-alloy shell with a pair of rocket pods attached to its sides. The snail smiled and spoke in a high-pitched, almost musical voice.

"Eetingsgroos Zearthlingspas! Earfoo otnoo! Zispa omecoo zinspa eacepoo!"

The humans were dumbfounded. "Uhh... Am I crazy or is that snail talking to us?" Captain Hawk stuttered.

"What did he say?" Snot asked.

"Zyouspas on'tdoo eakspoo Zuranusspa? Zispa antwoo elphoo zyouspas!" the snail said.

"Wait, I've heard that language before!" Agent Dare said. He reached into his pocket and pulled out a booklet titled *How to speak to Uranus; The Official CIA guide.* Agent Dare flipped through the pages. "He says he's here in peace, he wants to help us!"

"How can you tell?" Snot asked. Agent Dare tossed him the book.

"That's the official CIA guide for speaking with aliens. Uranus is the official language of the solar system. This snail speaks Uranus!"

"Uresoo odoo!" The snail replied. "Obatroos zattackedspa ymoo anetploo. Zispa antwoo otoo elphoo zyouspa opstoo emthoo."

"Snot can you translate?" Agent Dare asked. Snot flipped through the pages.

"My goodness, he says that RoBATs attacked his home planet. He wants to help us stop them!"

"Well, he sure saved our butts. I say welcome to the team." Agent Dare said. He gave the snail a friendly pat on the shell.

"I second the motion." Snot said. "He could be a huge help! What do we call him?"

"Ollarcoo."

"He says to check his collar." Snot said, glancing at the book. He read the label on the metal collar around the snail's neck.

"Space Lifeform from Uranus: Gastropod—Gets Extremely Radioactive. S-L-U-G-G-E-R . . . Slugger? His name is Slugger!"

Slugger nodded happily. "At'sthoo emoo!"

"Pleased to meet you, Slugger." Snot said. "I'm Snot Rocket, these are my friends, Agent Dare and Captain Hawk."

"We can't thank you enough for rescuing us. We would be neck-deep in RoBATs without your help." Captain Hawk said.

"Ymoo easureploo." Slugger said. "Ownoo, et'sloo indfoo Octordoo OseBleednoo, zispa ustjoo owknoo e'shoo ehindboo isthoo."

Agent Dare glanced at Snot. Snot translated. "He wants to find Doctor NoseBleed."

"We'd love to," Agent Dare said to Slugger, "but our helicopter is in bad shape. We can't get to Washington D.C. in that thing."

Slugger winked at the humans. "Onoo oblemproo. imbcloo zaboardspa!"

"What was that, Snot?" Agent Dare asked. Snot flipped a few pages and translated. "He says climb aboard. I think he has an idea!"

The humans climbed inside the helicopter and strapped in. Slugger crawled up on top where the rotors used to be. With his suction pad, he gripped the helicopter tight. "Oldhoo zonspa!"

"He says hold on!" Snot called out. Powerful purple flames fired from Slugger's rocket pods. The helicopter rattled, then lifted off from the ground.

Moments later, they were high in the air. Slugger used his rocket pods to fly them to Washington D.C. faster than ever.

"I don't know about you guys," Agent Dare said, "but I really like Slugger."

"You can say that again!" Snot replied.

***

One Hour Later, The White House, Washington D.C.

The helicopter sure looked bizarre. Slugger's titanium shell glittered in the sky like a gem. Bright purple flames burned as Slugger's rocket pods whooshed across the sky.

Hundreds of curious people watched as Slugger gently landed the helicopter on the White House lawn. Secret Service agents ran outside to see them. A dozen men in black suits and dark sunglasses stared dumbfounded at the creature on the grass. Agent Dare poked his head out the helicopter and waved to the Secret Service agents.

"Sorry we're late boys! We had a little engine trouble along the way," he said. Slugger crawled off the top of the helicopter.

"Whoa! Is that a snail?" one of the Secret Service men asked.

"It sure is funny looking," said another.

Slugger glared at them. "Zyouspa ookloo unnyfoo."

"Hey, what did that thing just say to me?" the Secret Service agent scowled. Snot quickly hid the guidebook behind his back. "Umm, he's just saying hello." he said with an awkward smile.

"I'm sure..." the Secret Service agent said. "Come along Mr. Rocket. The President is expecting you."

On their way inside, Snot nudged Slugger's shell. "That smart mouth of yours could get us in a lot of trouble you know."

"Ehoo artedstoo zitspa."

"Oh brother," Snot groaned.

Chapter 12: No Surrender!

Moments Later, The Oval Office, Washington D.C.

The Oval Office buzzed with excitement. General Guerra and President Hamm were working hard to come up with a rescue plan. Meanwhile, six tough-looking Space Marines inspected their equipment.

The Space Marines were an elite squad of men and women. Each was specially trained to perform dangerous search and rescue missions in outer space. They had a variety of high-tech equipment, including powerful jet-packs, laser widgets and solar gizmos.

The Space Marines snapped to attention when the Oval Office doors swung open.

President Hamm and General Guerra stopped what they were doing and smiled warmly at Snot and his friends. "Mr. Rocket, you're here just in time!" President Hamm said.

General Guerra saw Slugger and suddenly looked very surprised. "My goodness! What on Earth is that that thing?"

"I think you mean 'what on Uranus'," Snot Rocket said. "This is Slugger. He's a radioactive alien from the secret X-Machina base. After he escaped, he rescued us from Doctor NoseBleed's army of RoBATs."

"Alien you say?" General Guerra stroked his chin. The giant radioactive space-snail looked strange, but he was clearly very friendly. "Well, Slugger, I'm happy to have you on the team. We're going to need all the help we can get."

General Guerra's face became very serious. He lowered his voice, "Gentlemen, something terrible happened before you arrived. The scientists in the command center have all the details. This may be your most dangerous mission yet, Mr. Rocket."

General Guerra tapped a button on his desk. With a whoosh one of the oil paintings in the Oval Office whisked open to reveal a secret room.

"I'm afraid only humans can be allowed inside; Slugger's radioactivity might damage the equipment inside our command center. Can your extraterrestrial friend wait here?"

"Zohspa uresoo, avehoo zallspa ethoo unfoo ithoutwoo emoo."

"Don't worry Slugger, we'll be right out." Snot said. "Just don't get into any trouble while I'm gone."

"Onoo omiseproos." Slugger giggled.

Inside the secret command center, NASA scientists struggled to find a way to send the rescue team into space. Computers lined every wall.

But something was wrong.

The computers were showing nothing but gibberish! Numbers swirled like crazy on the screens. Simple equations flashed bright red ERROR signals. It was mathematical chaos.

"What happened here?" President Hamm asked.

One of the scientists stood from his seat, "We were preparing our final calculations to launch the rescue team into space. Then something terrible happened. There was a blinding flash of green light in the sky. Suddenly, our machines went haywire! Our calculators won't calculate, and our computers won't compute!"

"Holy smokes!" Agent Dare said, "The same thing happened to us today. It's what caused our helicopter to crash!"

"Mr. President," Snot Rocket said, "It looks like Doctor NoseBleed has found a way to destroy math. I don't know how, but it's the only explanation. Now he is terrorizing the planet with his secret weapon."

President Hamm went pale. "Good heavens. It all makes sense now." He looked to General Guerra. "What are our options, General? Is it possible to send Snot Rocket the Space Marines to the ISS without math?"

General Guerra shook his head grimly. "Without math, we won't be able to measure the distance from Earth to the Space Station. We could overshoot our target by mistake, and then the rescue team will get lost in space. Even if we get math working again, Doctor NoseBleed's *weapon of math destruction* is very concerning. It could hit our rocket and send it spiraling out of control! It's just too risky."

"Blast!" the President said. "And we can't look up the distance to the Space Station, because our internet was knocked out too."

A tear formed in the General Guerra's eye. "Our brave astronauts are being held prisoner, but we have no way to rescue them! Mr. President, it appears we have no choice but to surrender."

Everyone in the room gasped.

President Hamm slapped his desk. "We can't just surrender to that crazy cyborg! The fate of the free world is at stake!"

"But what else can we do?" A scientist asked.

"If there is a way to learn the distance from here to the Space Station," said the President, "then we still have a fighting chance."

"But how?" asked General Guerra. He looked across the room. Snot Rocket hadn't said much, which wasn't like him. "Snot," General Guerra said, "You've been awful quiet over there. What's on your mind?"

Snot was half the size of the grownups, but they all looked up to him for answers. Snot snapped his fingers. "I've got it! Before the internet was invented, where did people find important information?"

The grownups looked at each other.

President Hamm pulled out his smart phone and tried to look it up. "I don't know. I can't Google it!"

"Me either!" Agent Dare said, holding up his now useless smart phone. "Where did people find important information before the internet?"

Snot grinned. "Books!"

The grownup's jaws all dropped. "Books!" They exclaimed together. "Of course!"

"Mr. President, there's no time to lose. Do you have a phone?"

"Yes, our emergency phone still works. Who will you call?"

"Harry Pitts, Sir. He's my best friend, and he has the biggest collection of books I've ever seen. We're going to find a way to get to space. You have my word."

"Do you realize what this means?" Agent Dare asked.

General Guerra stood proudly. "It means there will be no surrender!"

Everyone cheered. "No surrender!"

Chapter 13: A Fortress in Space

Back at the ISS ...

Doctor NoseBleed was furious.

His RoBAT army failed to stop Snot Rocket. Even worse, his Weapon of Math Destruction accidentally unleashed a powerful alien from the X-Machina base. Now Doctor NoseBleed would have to fight his most dangerous rival *and* a giant radioactive space-snail.

"Give it up NoseBleed!" Patti Steal taunted. After her sneaky Tang attack, Doctor NoseBleed tied her and the other astronauts up extra tight. But she was still defiant. "Half of your RoBAT army is defeated. Now Snot Rocket will be up here any minute to rescue us!"

"Yes... yes I am sure he will..." Doctor NoseBleed said. He rubbed his chin and let out a cruel snicker. "If it's a fight he wants, then it's a fight he shall have! I still have enough RoBATs to finish the job." Doctor NoseBleed pulled out his special transmitter and pressed the button. "RoBAT army! Snot Rocket will be here soon, prepare to defend the Space Station."

Outside blinking red lights and flapping wings signaled the RoBATs' obedience.

"Soon Snot Rocket will arrive." Doctor NoseBleed hissed. "And he will have no choice but to face me. I will turn this Space Station into a fortress! No one will be able to stop me!"

"Ha!" Patti Steal said. "I'm going to enjoy watching Snot Rocket and his friends beat you, NoseBleed!"

"I told you, my name is _Doctor_ NoseBleed!!" he roared. At once his magnetic boot flew up and kicked the astronauts down the hallway. They all grunted in pain. Patti Steal tried to yell, but Doctor NoseBleed quickly pounced on them and taped their mouths shut.

"I am sick and tired of your insolence, Commander!" Doctor NoseBleed said. He gripped the bundle of captive astronauts with his metal claw. "Now that you can't speak, I think I have a use for you. I will lay the perfect trap, and _you_ shall be the bait! Muah Ha Ha!"

Outside, the RoBAT army swarmed around the Space Station to create a defensive perimeter. Doctor NoseBleed and his minions now had a fortress in space. All the astronauts could do was hope that Snot Rocket found them in time.

Chapter 14: Blast Off!!

Back on Earth...

Snot dialed a number on the President's emergency phone and eagerly waited for Harry Pitts to pick up.

"Hello?" a boy's voice answered.

"Harry, it's me!" Snot said.

"Snot? Oh boy am I happy to hear from you. Have you heard the news? Someone destroyed the Internet! Even worse, no one can get math to work anywhere. What's going on?"

"It's a *long* story, Harry." Snot said. "I'm here with the President of the United States, and we need your help. Do you still have your book about outer space?"

Harry was shocked when he heard about the President. But then again, his friend was always getting into all kinds of crazy situations. "Yes I still have it. It's my favorite book! What do you need?"

"Ok Harry," Snot began, "What's the distance from Earth to the International Space Station?"

Harry thought it was a strange question, but he trusted Snot Rocket. Harry found his book and flipped through the pages.

"Let's see... ok got it! Its 254 miles from here to the ISS."

"And how much power will it take to get us there?"

"Oh that's a tough one. Hold on..." Harry Pitts read the pages aloud. "To get into space, a rocket needs to produce enough power to pull away from Earth's gravity. That means it needs to push against the earth with enough force to break free. Like when you jump up from the ground, you are putting force against the Earth to go up in the air," he explained.

"The *Saturn Five* is one of NASA's most powerful rockets. It creates 7.6 *million* pounds of thrust! That is the same as 42 Boeing 747 jet planes pulling all at once! Wow, that's a crazy amount of power! Hey, why do you need information anyway?"

Snot took notes as Harry gave him the information. "I'll tell you as soon as this is all over. Right now I have to use this information to get to space."

"You have to do *what?*" Harry said, shocked. Suddenly, a woman's shrill voice started chattering in the background. "Uh-oh," Harry said. "Umm... Snot? Miz Rubble is here, and she's not happy."

"What else is new?" Snot groaned. Miz Rubble was always mad about something. "What does she say?"

"She says you'd better finish your science project on time."

"Can you tell her I'm going to space on an important mission?"

Harry repeated what Snot said, but Miz Rubble wasn't buying it. "Sorry Snot, she says she doesn't care *where* you're going, if your project is late, she's gonna give you a big fat F!"

"Oh brother." Snot said. "I'll do my best. Thanks for the help Harry!"

Snot hung up and took his notes to the President. "President Hamm, here's what my friend got for me. It's 254 miles to the Space Station, and it's going to take a lot of power to get us there."

"Can you use your Nuclear Nostril to launch the shuttle into space?"

Snot shook his head. "My Nuclear Nostril is powerful, but I can't launch a whole spaceship on my own. I'll need help."

"But who else can create their own rocket power?"

Right on cue, the President's words were cut off by the sound of a vase shattering in the Oval

Office. "Hey what's going on in there?" The President said.

Slugger was flying around the room like crazy. "EEWOO!!!" he said as he zipped around. *"Et'sloo ogoo otoo acespoo!"*

One of the Space Marines shrugged. "He just got excited and started flying around! We can't understand a word he's saying!"

Snot looked at his glowing, flying friend and got an idea. "Wait a minute. Maybe *I* can't make enough power on my own, but if Slugger uses his rockets too, it just might work! Slugger, are you ready to go to space?"

"Zi'mspa zallspa iredfoo zupspa! Et'sloo ogoo! EEWOO!!!"

"That sounds like a yes to me." President Hamm said with a smile. He then looked to Captain Hawk. "If Snot and Slugger launch the shuttle, can you fly it?" he asked.

Captain Hawk gave a crisp salute. "Absolutely! I've seen what Snot and Slugger can do. If they provide the power, I'll do the flying."

"And I'll be right beside you." Agent Dare said. "Snot Rocket, lead the way!"

Snot smiled. "Mr. President, it looks like we have a dream team."

President Hamm was pleased. "Everyone, it's almost time for lift-off. The fate of the world rests on your shoulders. I have full faith in each and every one of you. I'll see you on the launch pad!"

***

20 Minutes Later, at the Presidential Launch Pad

White puffs of steam hissed from all around the space shuttle. Slugger crawled on top of the space shuttle and gripped it tight with his suction pad. Purple flames sputtered everywhere as Slugger warmed up his rocket pods.

Inside, the Space Marines buckled up and prepared for launch.

Captain Hawk and Agent Dare were in the cockpit. When Captain Hawk was ready to fly, he waved to Snot. "We are ready for lift off!"

"Roger that," Snot answered. He was wearing a special space suit designed for a boy his height. His helmet was extra-large so his big nose would fit. The plan was simple. Snot took off his helmet and poked his head out of an open window on the space shuttle. Then he pulled a feather from his pocket.

"What's that for?" Agent Dare asked.

"Hold on tight; you're about to find out." Snot winked. "Are you ready, Slugger?"

"Zispa aswoo ornboo eadyroo!"

"Alright, start the countdown!"

Over the loudspeakers, President Hamm's voice echoed across the presidential launch pad. "Ten... Nine... Eight... Seven..."

Slugger fired his rocket pods with all his might. The space shuttle rattled and started to lift just slightly. The purple flames burned brighter than ever. Meanwhile, Snot tickled his nuclear nostril with the feather. Then his nose scrunched up.

President Hamm gave one last salute. "Blast off!"

"AHHH CHOOO!!!!!"

Snot's sneeze unleashed tremendous power. The blast from his Nuclear Nostril was so strong that everyone aboard the shuttle was thrown back in their seats. Snot and Slugger launched them faster than any rocket had gone before!

Once they were clear of the launch pad, Snot quickly ducked inside the space shuttle. Before they left the atmosphere, Snot put on his helmet and sealed the window shut. "Alright Slugger," Snot said over the radio, "I gave us a pretty good boost. Now take us to the Space Station!"

"Zayespa-Zayespa Otsnoo!"

Chapter 15: Rescue Mission

At the ISS...

On the Space Station, Doctor NoseBleed twisted a wrench against the WMD. It wasn't long before the evil laser was repaired. Even worse, he added a nasty surprise for Snot Rocket.

The WMD was fully armed, and it was packing a dirty trick too. Doctor NoseBleed hit the ignition sequence. "Yes, now I can destroy all of the math on the planet! The world will have no choice but to hail me as their overlord."

He fired laser fired at Earth. It wrapped the entire planet in a green orb. All over the world, math ceased to exist.

Doctor NoseBleed snickered. It was only a matter of time before all of humanity begged him for mercy. Victory was so close, he could almost taste it.

Bright purple light caught Doctor NoseBleed's eye. He glared at the approaching space shuttle. Then he let out a wicked laugh. "Aha! Our guests have arrived. RoBATs! The time for battle is now, *attack!*"

A hundred RoBATs swarmed into battle formations. The wicked machines charged at the approaching space shuttle. Doctor NoseBleed whipped his cape over his shoulder and hurried inside the Space Station.

Aboard the space shuttle, the rescuers got ready to fight.

"Incoming!" Snot called out. Alarms blared in the space shuttle. The Space Marines fired up their jet-packs and grabbed their laser widgets. Slugger bravely held onto the space shuttle and guided them closer to the ISS.

"Keep it up, Slugger!" Snot said, "Get us nice and close. The Space Marines will fight off the RoBATs and I'll rescue the astronauts."

"Here they come!" Agent Dare shouted.

The first wave of RoBATs swooped in. Snot flew forward with his jet pack to lead the fight. He kicked the first RoBAT in the charge. Another RoBAT took its place, but Snot quickly knocked it down too.

"Fire the laser widgets!" Agent Dare said to the Space Marines. "Aim for the antennas on their heads! Charge!"

Six Space Marines fired their laser widgets. Red laser beams flew in every direction. RoBAT's exploded every time a laser hit one of their antennas. But Doctor NoseBleed's army had a few tricks of their own. Forming a giant V, they flew down and crashed into the Space Marines.

"Hold your formation!" a Space Marine yelled. She blasted a RoBAT with her laser widget.

"Nice shot!" Snot said.

"We'll hold them off as long as we can," the Space Marine said. "Go get the astronauts, hurry!"

Snot gave her a salute and flew toward the Space Station.

While the battle between the RoBATs and the Space Marines raged on, Snot spotted the weapon of math destruction. "Wow, that thing is huge," he whispered aloud. Snot let out a burst from his jet pack and flew closer.

Beneath the WMD was an open hatch. It led right inside the ISS. Snot thought it was strange. *Hmm... that seems almost too easy* he thought.

Despite his suspicion that something was wrong, there was no time to waste. Snot quickly flew through the open hatch.

Once he was in the Space Station, the hatch automatically slammed shut with a *bang!*

Chapter 16: It's a Trap!

Inside the Space Station...

It was quiet.

Too quiet.

Snot activated his magnetic boots and landed on the ground. He walked along the hallways and searched for the astronauts. Also, he kept a sharp eye out for any sign of Doctor NoseBleed. That cyborg always had a sneaky, evil plan.

"Hello? Can anyone hear me?" Snot called out. "My name is Snot Rocket, I'm here to rescue you! Hellooo?"

His voiced echoed inside the empty Space Station. Snot felt a chill run down his spine. Something didn't feel right.

A metallic *clang* echoed from down the hall. "Hello?" Snot said. He ran toward the sound. He turned a corner and saw all three of the astronauts. They were tied up, but they were safe!

Snot rushed to untie them. "I'm glad you're all ok! I have a space shuttle waiting outside."

The astronauts seemed very afraid. They all tried to shout something, but their mouths were all taped shut.

"It's ok everyone, I'm here to help you." Snot said. He pulled the tape from Patti Steal's lips. Her eyes went wide with fear.

"You have to get out of here! It's a trap!"

Right on cue, all the lights in the Space Station went out. Metal boots stomped across the floor.

Clang! Clang! Clang!

Snot turned on his heels. Down the hall, a bright red eye glowed in the dark. A deep, frightening voice boomed.

"Snot Rocket..." the evil cyborg said. "How kind of you to join me."

"Let them go Doctor NoseBleed. It's me you want isn't it? Release the astronauts!"

Doctor NoseBleed laughed. "You fool, can't you see it's too late? My weapon of math destruction is fully armed now. All that stands in my way is one little boy with a big nose." Doctor NoseBleed made a fist with his robot claw. Snot bravely stood in front of the astronauts to protect them.

"This is your last chance to give up Doctor NoseBleed!" Snot said.

Doctor NoseBleed lunged at Snot Rocket.

"RAWRRRR!!!"

Chapter 17: The Final Battle

"Snot, look out!" Patti Steal yelled.

Doctor NoseBleed threw a punch with his massive robot claw. Snot activated his jetpack. There was a burst of orange light as Snot shot up to avoid being hit. Doctor NoseBleed's claw crashed into the ground—completely missing his target.

Now Snot had the advantage. Hovering in the air with his jetpack, he kicked Doctor NoseBleed square in the face.

"Arrggh!" Doctor NoseBleed roared. His robot claw whipped up and smacked Snot right out of the air like a fly. There was a *smash!* as Snot crashed into the wall.

"You're just a child, Snot Rocket. You're no match for me! Muah Ha Ha!"

Snot quickly got to his feet. "Dynamite comes in small packages," he said. He and Doctor NoseBleed ran toward each other. Snot activated his jetpack again. Shooting forward like a missile, Snot punched Doctor NoseBleed right in the face.

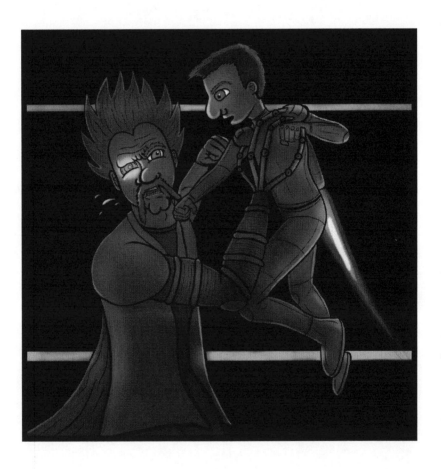

"Ooomph!" NoseBleed grunted. He stumbled back from the impact. He swung his claw, but Snot ducked just in time.

"That's right, let him have it!" the astronauts cheered. Snot fired up his jet pack and threw himself at Doctor NoseBleed to tackle him. The next thing Snot saw was Doctor NoseBleed's metal boot kicking up toward his face.

Bang!

Snot didn't have time to react. Doctor NoseBleed's boot kicked Snot so hard that he flew back and dented the wall behind him.

Snot tried to shake it off. "Wow, that evil cyborg is strong!" he grunted under his breath. "This might be harder than I thought.

"I can do this all day!" Doctor NoseBleed taunted. "Is that all you've got, boy?"

"Come on Snot, get up! You can beat him!" Patti Steal said.

"I have heard enough from you!" Doctor NoseBleed said. He reached out and hit a big red **JETTISON** button. Alarms blared. Red lights flashed. A door at the far end of the Space Station swung open.

Air rushed out with the force of a hurricane. The astronauts tumbled helplessly toward the open door. If they fell out into space, they would surely die.

"No!" Snot yelled. Without thinking of his own safety, he jumped toward the astronauts. Snot activated his jetpack for an extra boost.

Without a second to spare, he caught the astronauts and pulled them away from the hole that led to space.

But there was still danger. All the air was being sucked out of the Space Station. Within a few seconds, it would become impossible to breathe.

"We need to get to the escape pod!" Patti Steal yelled. "It's the only way we can survive!"

"Where is it?" Snot asked.

Patti Steal nodded toward a small, circular door in the hallway. "It's behind that hatch, hurry!"

Using all his strength, Snot pulled the astronauts to escape pod where they would be safe. He then worked quickly to open the hatch.

Meanwhile, metal boots thumped against the ground; Doctor NoseBleed was getting close.

"He's coming for us again!" Igor Popov yelled.

"If he wants to get to you, he'll have to get through me first!" Snot promised them. He pushed the astronauts inside the escape pod and locked the door. Snot then pressed the big green **OXYGEN** button. There was a loud hiss, and the escape pod quickly filled with air for the astronauts to breathe.

"You'll be safe here. Hold on!" Snot said. He tried to jettison the escape pod, but Doctor NoseBleed finally caught up with him.

The metal claw latched onto Snot's ankle. Snot tried to pull away, but Doctor NoseBleed was too strong.

"It's been fun, Snot Rocket, but I have a planet to conquer." He said. Then he started swinging Snot around in circles.

"Whoaaaa!" Snot yelled.

"See you on the other side!" Doctor NoseBleed laughed. He released his grip on Snot's ankle—sending Snot flying across the Space Station.

Snot flew down the hall and smashed into the wall so hard that his body went straight through it. Without gravity, Snot nearly tumbled out into space. Fortunately, he was able to activate his magnetic boots just in time. Snot stuck to the outer hull of the Space Station at the last instant.

"Sorry NoseBleed," Snot winked. "But I think I'll stick around a little longer!"

Doctor NoseBleed growled angrily; this defiant little human was becoming a real pain in the neck. He hurried out of the Space Station to continue the showdown with his hated rival.

Snot took a second to check on his friends.

All around him, Agent Dare and the Space Marines were bravely battling the RoBAT army. Lasers and explosions filled the sky. With all the commotion, it was impossible to tell who was winning the battle. Before Snot could ask his friends if they needed help, a huge claw punched through the hull of the Space Station.

Doctor NoseBleed leaped out and landed right in front of him.

Thump! Thump! Thump!

Heavy boots stomped closer and closer toward Snot. He tried to activate his jetpack to fly away, but it only sparked. The crash through the wall did more damage than Snot realized. Snot quickly unsnapped his broken jet pack and let it float away.

"Muah Ha Ha!" Doctor NoseBleed laughed. He kicked Snot Rocket before the boy had a chance to fight back. Snot got up to his knees, but Doctor NoseBleed kicked him again.

Slugger saw that Snot was in trouble. Activating his rocket pods, he flew away from the space shuttle and rushed to help his friend. "Oldhoo onspa Otsnoo!" he yelled. "Zi'mpsa omincoo!"

"No Slugger, it's too dangerous!" Snot warned.

Slugger ignored him. The brave space-snail flew at Doctor NoseBleed with all his power, but the evil cyborg was ready. Doctor NoseBleed caught Slugger with his metal claw. He then cocked his arm back and threw Slugger toward the army of RoBATs.

"How about a nice game of catch?" Doctor NoseBleed shouted.

"Zouchpaaaa!" Slugger screamed. The RoBATs caught Slugger by the shell and started bouncing him around like a ball.

Things went from bad to worse. When Snot got back to his feet, he saw that the Space Marines were completely surrounded.

"Pull back! Pull back!" Agent Dare said. He and the Space Marines fired their laser widgets to cover their retreat, but the RoBATs were hot on their trail.

Doctor NoseBleed laughed. "It's over Snot Rocket. Surrender now and perhaps I will spare your friends!"

"Never." Snot coughed. "You can beat me up all you want. I'll never surrender."

"Very well..." Doctor NoseBleed grinned. "RoBATs! Finish them off!"

Screeching, swarming wings fluttered everywhere. The RoBATs began their final attack. Snot knew the mission would fail if he didn't do something soon. They needed a miracle to defeat Doctor NoseBleed now!

Chapter 18: One Last Chance to Save the World

Things could not have been worse for Snot Rocket.

The Weapon of Math Destruction glowed brighter than ever. Earth was completely surrounded with eerie green light. The Space Marines were in full retreat. Slugger tried to help, but the RoBATs punted him around like a hacky-sack.

Doctor NoseBleed threw back his head and laughed. "Aha! Victory is finally mine!"

Snot couldn't give up. Too many people were counting on him. His head hurt. His body ached. But he was brave and he knew what he had to do.

There was just one last chance to save the world.

Snot grasped the sides of his space helmet. With a quarter-turn, he unlocked the helmet from his suit.

"Snot what are you doing!?" Agent Dare yelled over the radio. "Don't take off your helmet! You could die!"

Snot ignored him. Too many people needed his help. He had to take a risk.

"You crazy fool!" Doctor NoseBleed said. "You are only human, you'll suffocate!"

"That's a chance I'll have to take." Snot said. He pulled off his helmet and let it float away into space.

To everyone's surprise, nothing happened. Snot didn't suffocate. Even weirder, he could breathe just fine!

"How is that possible??" Doctor NoseBleed gasped. "You should be dead!"

"I'm as surprised as you are..." Snot said quietly. He took a deep breath through his nose. Somehow, he could breathe in space!

Doctor NoseBleed glared at him. "It's your Nuclear Nostril, it must be! It's the source of all your powers..."

"Looks like I'm full of surprises today." Snot grinned.

"After I defeat you, I'll take your nose as a trophy. Then I'll use its powers for myself!"

"But first you have to take it." Snot taunted. He reached into his pocket and whipped out his special feather. Snot held it out like a sword and waved it in front of him.

Doctor NoseBleed stopped in his tracks. "A feather?" he laughed. "The mighty Snot Rocket brought only a feather into battle? Ha! Pounding you into mush will be easier than I thought!"

"Bring it on!"

The evil cyborg charged at him. Snot jumped back. Before Doctor NoseBleed could reach him, he quickly flicked the feather against his Nuclear Nostril.

His nose tingled and twitched. A sneeze was coming – a BIG one!

"E'shoo onnagoo owbloo!" Slugger yelled. He retreated into his shell for cover. All the Space Marines flew behind the shuttle.

Captain Hawk saw what was happening and quickly steered the space shuttle away from the blast zone. "Hold on everyone, Snot's gonna sneeze!!"

Doctor NoseBleed's jaw dropped. "Oh no!"

He tried to run, but it was too late. Snot Rocket aimed his nose right at him.

"AHHH CHOOO!!!"

It was the most powerful sneeze of all time. A blinding flash of light lit up the ISS. The explosion was so big that even people on Earth had to shield their eyes from its brightness.

There was a gut-shaking *BOOM!*

The sneeze blasted Doctor NoseBleed off of the Space Station as if he were just a fly. "Noooo!!!!" he screamed. The explosion sent Doctor NoseBleed far, far into deep space until he was just another twinkle of light among the stars.

The RoBATs were blown to pieces. Springs, bolts, and broken wings floated all around. With one tremendous blast of power, Snot had destroyed the RoBATs and their evil leader all at once.

Slugger popped his head out of his shell.

"Olyhoo okessmo. Atthoo aswoo zawesomespa!"

Smoke was still puffing out from Snot Rocket's nose. "Thanks Slugger, is everyone okay?"

"We're more than okay." A Space Marine said. "We have won the battle!"

Agent Dare pumped his fist with delight. "Snot Rocket has defeated the evil Doctor NoseBleed!" he declared.

Everyone cheered, except for Snot Rocket.

"At'swhoo ongwroo?" Slugger asked

Snot wiped his nose and looked at the giant laser beam attached to the ISS. It was still glowing bright.

"That thing is still destroying all the math on Earth. We have to stop it!"

Chapter 19: Doctor Nosebleed's Revenge

There was still work to be done.

The green laser from the WMD was glowing brighter than ever. Its beam held all of humanity hostage in a math-less world. Chaos reigned down on Earth, as even the most basic math tools went bonkers.

"We have to disarm the weapon of math destruction!" Snot said. "Captain Hawk, get ready to fly back to Earth."

"Aye Aye Snot!" Captain Hawk said.

"Slugger, after I disable the WMD, I'll need you to carry the escape pod."

"Oodgoo zideaspa!"

Snot got to work right away. He ran to the WMD. It was an evil-looking device. Spikes covered its surface and strange wires sprawled out like spider webs. Green light glowed against Snot Rocket's face. He found the control panel and searched for a way to shut down the laser.

"It's locked!" Snot said. Doctor NoseBleed programed the WMD with a secret sequence, one only a true math genius could crack. Without the code, there was no way to shut down the WMD. Four numbers glowed red on the control panel, followed by two empty spaces.

03	03	06	09	☐	☐

Agent Dare looked at the strange sequence and shook his head. "That doesn't make sense. They seem like random numbers! Can you crack the code?"

"I might..." Snot said. He pulled out a pencil and note pad and got to work.

"What are you doing?" Agent Dare asked.

"They aren't just random numbers; Doctor NoseBleed is too smart for that. These numbers have something in common; and I think I have an idea what it is. What's three plus three?"

"That's easy, six," Agent Dare said.

"Right, and the code is three, three, six. The next number is nine. But look! What do you get when you add the two numbers before it?"

"Well, that's three plus six, so nine. Wow, that's quite a coincidence! But I don't understand how it helps."

Snot Rocket checked his math. He was sure that he knew the answer to Doctor NoseBleed arithmetic riddle.

"Doctor NoseBleed is clever; he used a special code called the Fibonacci sequence! Do you see? Each number in the code is the sum of the two numbers before it." Snot smiled and wrote down some calculations on his notepad. "Three plus three is six, three plus six is nine, so the next number in the code will be six plus nine ... that's fifteen!"

Snot typed 15 into Doctor NoseBleed's control panel. To everyone's surprise, the number worked!

"That's amazing, you've cracked the code! So what's the next number?" Agent Dare asked.

"The next number will be the sum of the two before it, so fifteen plus nine, that's 24!"

Snot typed the number 24 into the keypad. When he hit the **ENTER** key, the green laser vanished!

Slowly, all the machines on Earth hummed back to life. Blank screens shined bright as the Internet came back online. Math all over the world was back! Doctor NoseBleed's evil plan for a math-less world was officially defeated.

"He did it! Snot Rocket saved the world!" the Space Marines cheered.

"Zyou'respa ethoo estboo Otsnoo!" Slugger smiled.

"Wait..." Snot said, looking down at the control panel. "Something's wrong."

The control panel sparked back to life. Agent Dare looked at Snot. "What's going on?"

Green light burst from the WMD again. Only this time, it glowed right above the Space Station. The light flashed several times until a hologram of Doctor NoseBleed's face appeared like a digital ghost.

"Aha! Snot Rocket..." the hologram said in a scratchy, echoing voice. "It appears you have cracked my secret code, as I knew you would..."

Snot felt his stomach tighten up with dread. *As he knew I would?* Snot suddenly had a very, very bad feeling.

The hologram continued, "I prepared a little surprise for you, just in case you found a way to beat me. Now *I* shall have the last laugh! Goodbye, Snot Rocket! Muah Ha Ha! *Muah HA HA!!!*"

The hologram faded away, but Doctor NoseBleed's evil laugh continued.

"What's going on?" a Space Marine asked. She could tell this was bad news. As if to answer her question, red letters flashed on the WMD control screen.

WARNING! WARNING!

SELF DESTRUCT SEQUENCE INITIATED!

DETONATION IN 20...19...18...

Snot waved his arms wildly to get everyone's attention. "Doctor NoseBleed programmed the WMD to self-destruct! It's gonna explode in less than twenty seconds!"

Chapter 20: The Final Countdown

Agent Dare fired up his jet pack and got ready to evacuate. "Snot we have to get out of here! That thing is gonna destroy the whole Space Station!"

"I'm not leaving without the astronauts." Snot said. "I'm going back for them!"

"There's no time!" Agent Dare shouted.

"I have to try!"

"Zi'mspa omingcoo ithwoo zyouspa!" Slugger said. He flew down to the Space Station to help Snot with the rescue.

The clock was ticking. Captain Hawk, Agent Dare and the Space Marines hurried to escape the danger zone. Meanwhile, Snot and Slugger raced toward the astronauts.

17...16...15...

Snot's magnetic boots thumped faster and faster as he ran to the escape pod. Purple flames from Slugger's rocket pods lit up the dark halls as the space-snail stayed hot on Snot's trail.

When Snot made it to the escape pod, he could see the astronauts were still trapped inside. He banged against the window to get their attention.

"You came back for us!" Patti Steal exclaimed. "Thank you, Snot!"

"Don't thank me just yet. Doctor NoseBleed set a trap. This whole place will be destroyed in a few seconds."

"Oh no!" Igor Popov and Yung Li gasped.

"Don't panic, I'm not leaving without you." Snot promised. "Is there a way to get you out of here?"

Patti Steal nodded. "You'll need to jettison the escape pod. It's the only way to get us to safety in time," she said. She then pointed over Snot's shoulder. "Over there! Hit the big red jettison button—then stand back! It will activate rockets to release us from the Space Station."

The radio on Snot's space suit crackled. Captain Hawk spoke to him over the speakers. "The Space Marines are safely aboard the shuttle," he said. "But you have to hurry! There's only fourteen seconds left on the timer!"

"Roger that!" Snot said. He looked at Slugger. "You heard him! We'll be cutting this *real* close. Can

97

you attach yourself to the escape pod and fly them out of here?"

"Ateverwhoo ewoo odoo, zitspa ashoo otoo eboo astfoo!"

"Good." Snot said. He found the red **JETTISON** button and slammed it hard. White steam hissed all around him. The escape pod started to float away, but then it got jammed!

The Space Station was seriously damaged during the battle against Doctor NoseBleed and his RoBATs. Loose cables and broken equipment lay everywhere. The escape pod was tangled in a mess of debris.

"We're stuck!" Patti Steal yelled. "Just go on without us, it's too late!"

10...9...8...

Snot knew he was running out of time, but he ignored Patti Steal's demands that he save himself. He searched around to find a way to release the pod, but it was hopelessly stuck. Snot pulled and pushed with all his might, but the escape pod would not budge.

"So much for Plan A, time to try Plan B!" Snot said.

"What's Plan B?" Patti Steal asked.

"Brace yourselves; you're about to find out!" Snot said.

Snot aimed his nose at the cables and debris that were keeping the escape pod trapped. There was just one way to break the astronauts free in time—and it was very risky!

Snot Rocket warmed up his Nuclear Nostril.

Patti told her crew to buckle up. "He's about to use his Booger Blaster, hold on tight everyone!"

Snot aimed his nose at the escape pod and fired his most powerful Booger Blaster yet. *BOOM!*

7...6...5...

Huge chunks of metal and pieces of space debris flew everywhere. Then the escape pod started to float away. It worked! The astronauts were free!

"Slugger, grab them and go straight to Earth, I'll meet you there!"

"Oodgoo uckloo Otsnoo, Zispa on'twoo etloo zyouspa owndoo!"

Slugger attached himself to the escape pod and let out a long burst of flame. In a flash he was gone. Meanwhile, the Space Marines clamored into the space shuttle. Captain Hawk looked worried.

"I don't have enough power to escape the explosion, help us Snot!" Captain Hawk said.

Snot pulled out his lucky feather. "Hold on tight everyone, I'm gonna sneeze us back to Earth."

He jumped up to the space shuttle and held on tight. Then he tickled his nuclear nostril.

***

Slugger was worried. He looked back to see how Snot and the humans were doing. Snot was tickling his Nuclear Nostril—trying his best to work up a sneeze powerful enough to launch the shuttle to safety.

Then Slugger saw the countdown on the WMD.

3...2...1...

SELF DESTRUCT INITIATED!

Bright green light burst from the WMD. Slugger watched with horror as a massive explosion seemed to wrap all around Snot Rocket and the humans.

"Zohspa onoo!" Slugger cried.

Chapter 21: Home, Sweet Home!

The explosion from Doctor NoseBleed's trap was so powerful that even people down on Earth could hear the blast. A tremendous green flash lit up the sky.

President Hamm and General Guerra ran onto the White House lawn and looked up. They had to shield their eyes from the brightness of the green flash.

"What happened up there?" President Hamm asked.

"Doctor NoseBleed must have rigged his WMD with a self-destruct program. He knew Snot Rocket would probably beat him, so he set a trap."

"That explosion is humongous!"

General Guerra looked very sad. "Snot Rocket is a special boy. But I don't see how even a super hero like him could survive such a violent explosion."

President Hamm fell silent for a few moments. Snot was incredibly brave. Too brave. The young hero was willing to sacrifice himself to save the planet from Doctor NoseBleed. "We owe Snot Rocket a tremendous debt of gratitude." President Hamm said.

"Wait a minute, what's that?" General Guerra said. He pointed up to a bright purple speck in the sky. Like a meteor, it grew bigger and brighter with each passing second. General Guerra held up a pair of binoculars. "Uhh... Mr. President, you're not gonna believe this."

He handed over the binoculars. "Is that a flying snail?"

General Guerra let out a whoop. "It's Slugger! And he's holding an escape pod with the astronauts inside. Look, that's Snot Rocket flying behind him! They made it! My goodness they made it!"

"That young man is full of surprises." President Hamm said. He smiled for a moment. The President took a long look at the incoming spacecraft, then realized that an impact was coming. He backed up nervously. "Hey... do you think they're coming in a bit fast?"

General Guerra's eyes went wide. "Yeah... and they're headed straight for us!"

President Hamm and General Guerra scrambled to get out of the landing zone. President

Hamm shouted to the Secret Service agents on the lawn, "Everyone get out of the way! They're coming in hot!"

"You heard the President, move it people!" General Guerra yelled.

"Ookloo zoutspa!" Slugger yelled.

The ground shook like an earthquake when Slugger crash-landed. A huge cloud of dust shot up as he and the escape pod with the astronauts skidded to a stop on the lawn. Seconds later, Snot Rocket came crashing down too. He was riding on top of the space shuttle like a cowboy on a bucking bronco.

"Look out!" Snot yelled. "I don't have any brakes on this thing!"

There was a huge *BOOM* as Snot and the shuttle hit the ground. "Whooaaaa!!!" all the Space Marines inside the shuttle howled.

They slid to a stop right beside Slugger and the astronauts. Smoke and steam hung all around them like a cloud. Snot's hairs were singed, and his space suit was badly damaged, but he wasn't hurt! He escaped Doctor NoseBleed's trap just in time.

President Hamm was first to rush out onto the White House lawn to greet them. "Snot my boy! You've done it!"

Patti Steal, Igor Popov, and Yung Li emerged from the escape pod. "Three cheers for our hero,

Snot Rocket!" Patti Steal said with a smile. "Hip-hip!"

"Hooray!"

"Hip-hip!"

"Hooray!"

"Hip-hip!"

"Hooray!"

The astronauts, the Space Marines, the President, and General Guerra all erupted in applause. Snot hopped down from the space shuttle and smiled. "I couldn't have done it without Slugger and the Space Marines!"

The President smiled. "Always humble. That's one of the things I like best about you." President Hamm reached into his coat pocket and pulled out two rocket-shaped medals. He then waved to the crowd of people gathering around the White House lawn.

"If I could have everyone's attention, please?" he began. "Early this morning, I received the terrible news that our astronauts were being held hostage. Worse yet, I learned that the dastardly, no-good Doctor NoseBleed was plotting world domination. Things seemed bleak..."

The crowd fell into awed silence as the president turned to face Snot Rocket and Slugger. "But no matter how bad things looked, these two heroes showed incredible gallantry. Doctor NoseBleed is defeated, the RoBAT army is no more, and our astronauts are safe at home." He held up the rocket-shaped medals so all the people in the crowd and the flashing cameras could get a good look.

"The United States of America can't thank you enough for your courage today. It is my pleasure to present to you these Medals for Galactic Gallantry."

He handed the medals to General Guerra. General Guerra saluted Snot and Slugger and placed the medals around their necks. There was tremendous applause from the crowd. Slugger got so excited that he jumped up and down.

"Ankthoo zyouspas, ankthoo zyouspas eryvoo uchmoo!"

"Thank you everyone. I was just doing my duty!" Snot said.

President Hamm patted Snot on the shoulder. "What you did today was nothing short of amazing. Should you ever need anything, you can give my office a call. I owe you big time, kid."

"That goes extra for the CIA." Agent Dare said with a big smile. "Thanks for saving my life back there. You can call me anytime."

Snot blushed a little. He was about to say that no thanks was necessary, but he was interrupted when the President's phone started ringing.

"This is the President." He answered. "Yes... yes he's right here..." he handed the phone to Snot Rocket. "It's for you."

Snot looked puzzled when he took the phone. Who could be calling him now?

"Hello?"

Harry Pitts was on the other end. "Snot, it's me," he said. "Where are you? The Science Fair started half an hour ago! Miz Rubble is gonna give you a big fat F if you don't get here soon!"

"Oh shoot! I forgot about the Science Fair!" Snot exclaimed. "Stall her as long as you can. I'm on my way, and I have my project with me."

"Just hurry!" Harry said.

"Wow, that teacher of yours is strict," President Hamm said. "Surely saving the world is a fair excuse?"

Snot laughed. "Not for Miz Rubble. Thanks for awarding me the Medal for Galactic Gallantry, but I have to run!"

"At'swhoo zyourspa ojectproo?" Slugger asked.

Snot winked at him. "_You're_ my project. Come on Slugger!"

Slugger rolled his eyes. "Zohspa otherbroo."

Chapter 22: Science Fair

The mood in the gymnasium at Evergreen Elementary School was very different from the happy crowds in Washington D.C.

Science presentations about space and the galaxy were lined up in neat rows. The kids did their best, they really did, but nothing was good enough for Miz Rubble. Her red pen was hard at work scribbling down one F after another. As she stomped up along the rows of presentations, she left a trail of spooked and sobbing children in her wake.

"Too sloppy!" she screeched to one student.

"Not creative enough!" she said to another.

"Ugh, this one is *too* creative!" she hollered. Just like that, Miz Rubble handed out three F's in a row!

"She is ruthless today." Harry Pitts muttered. He glanced nervously at the empty presentation booth next to his. A piece of paper marked the booth as Snot Rocket's, but he was nowhere to be seen. *Oh boy, I hope he gets here soon!* Harry worried.

"What is the meaning of this?" Miz Rubble barked at Harry. She appeared so suddenly that Harry jumped in surprise.

"M-Miz Rubble! My project is about the solar system." He stuttered. "As you can see, I made a scale model of the eight planets and their moons—

"I am not talking about your project!" Miz Rubble interrupted. "Where is Mr. Rocket? I warned him a dozen times not to be late today!"

Harry shrugged. "I don't know... he said something about a mission in space. I'm sure he'll be here any minute."

Miz Rubble huffed. "Hogwash!" she declared. "Harry, your planets are too round! That's a D minus for you! As for Snot Rocket..."

The gymnasium doors flew open before she finished her sentence. Miz Rubble turned to see what the commotion was about. She nearly leaped from her shoes when she saw Snot Rocket standing in the doorway. He was wearing the most bizarre outfit. It looked like a NASA space suit, but it was ripped and burned in many places, as if it had been through some kind of battle. Also peculiar, Snot had a shiny, rocket-shaped medal hanging around his neck.

"I'm here! And I have my project!" Snot declared.

Miz Rubble put her hands on her hips and glared at Snot.

"You're an hour late! This science project had better be quite impressive." She pulled out her big red pen and removed the cap.

"Oh it is, believe me." Snot said with a grin. He turned to face his classmates, who were all shocked to see Snot wearing such bizarre clothes. "Boys and girls of Evergreen Elementary, I have made perhaps the most important scientific discovery of our time. I have discovered proof of intelligent life on other planets!"

Miz Rubble raised a suspicious eyebrow. "Aliens? You expect me to believe you have proof of aliens?"

Snot put his fingers to his lips and let out a high whistle. "Slugger! Come in here and meet everybody!"

The sound of rockets echoed outside.

"Zi'mspa erehoo!" Slugger squealed. He zipped through the open door like a flying cannon ball. The entire gymnasium shined blue and purpled from his radioactive glow. There was a puff of smoke and Slugger landed right at Miz Rubble's feet.

Miz Rubble was dumbfounded. Her jaw hung agape and her eyes were as big as baseballs. "What on Earth?" she stuttered.

"I think you mean 'What on your Uranus?'" Snot corrected her. "This is Slugger. He is a Space Lifeform from Uranus, Gastropod, that Gets Extremely Radioactive."

"Owhoo odoo zyouspa odoo?" Slugger smiled.

Miz Rubble jumped in surprise.

"Yikes! That thing talks?"

"Sure does," Snot answered. "He speaks Uranus, which I recently learned is the official language of our solar system. He's friendly too!"

Miz Rubble struggled to find words. A real alien was sitting right in front of her eyes. It was amazing, stunning, she couldn't believe it, but her shock soon faded. Miz Rubble's infamous glare soon returned.

"Enough!" Miz Rubble declared. Her thin arms waved all around as she yelled at Snot. "Coming in here late, dressed like some sort of spaceman, ranting and raving about aliens from Uranus. I will not stand for this nonsense!"

She whipped out her pen and scribbled a giant red F by Snot's name. "Too fantastic! Too groundbreaking! F minus, double F minus!"

Miz Rubble was out of breath when she finished her tirade. Huffing and puffing, she turned to leave Snot and Slugger by the empty booth.

"Iddoo zyouspa earhoo atthoo? Eshoo ayssoo Zi'mspa ootoo antasticfoo." Slugger said.

"I'm glad you see the bright side," Snot groaned. "I just failed science class."

Snot slumped his shoulders and started to leave. But a high pitched *ringgg!!* echoed throughout the gymnasium.

It was Miz Rubble's phone. "Who is this?" she demanded when she answered. "You'd better have a good reason for interrupting . . . oh . . . oh yes I see . . ."

Miz Rubble's cruel expression melted away. Her face turned pale and she looked at Snot. "Yes... yes of course... I understand..." she stammered. She waited for the other person to hang up before she put her phone away. Miz Rubble looked as though she'd seen a ghost.

"Are you okay, Miz Rubble? Who was that?" Snot asked.

Miz Rubble was totally shocked. "That was the President of the United States..." she said quietly, "He says that you get an A plus."

Miz Rubble pulled out her never-before-used blue pen and scratched out the F by Snot's name. Beside it she wrote: *By order of the President, A+*

"Zyayspa!" Slugger cheered.

"You said it, Slugger!" Snot smiled. The two pals jumped in the air in delight.

Things were truly great. Snot Rocket saved the day yet again, and now he had a new friend to help him on his missions. Where would Snot's adventures take him next? Only time could tell. One thing was for sure, he could always count on his friends to help him succeed.

Memo to all CIA Agents,

> Humans are not alone in the universe. Beyond Earth, there are over 100 billion intelligent aliens in our solar system.

> Most aliens speak Uranus. All CIA agents must be able to communicate with these aliens. It is vital to national security that all CIA agents learn to read, write, and speak Uranus.

> Fortunately, Uranus is very similar to English. By following these simple rules, CIA agents will quickly become fluent in Uranus.

<u>Rules for Speaking Uranus</u>

(1) When a word begins with a consonant or a pair of consonants, move those letters to the end of the word.

(2) Next, add "oo" to the end. If the word is plural, add "oos"

>> *EXAMPLE*: Rockets → Ocketsroos

>> *EXAMPLE*: Train → Aintroo

(3) When a word begins with a vowel (including "y"), add "z" to the beginning of the word.

(4) Next, add "spa" to the end of the word. If the word is plural, add "spas"

>> *EXAMPLE*: Uranus → Zuranusspa

>> *EXAMPLE*: Apples → Zapplesspas

(5) Now that you know the rules, can you decode these messages? An important clue to Snot's next adventure is hidden inside!

(a) Otsnoo Ocketroo zisspa zaspa avebroo oyboo. Ishoo extnoo zadventurespa illwoo eboo zinspa Zegyptspa!

(b) Etgoo eadyroo orfoo oremoo zactionspa, enwhoo Otsnoo ightsfoo zanspa zancientspa ursecoo!

Can't Get Enough Snot Rocket?

There's a whole universe waiting for you online!

Explore full color images, get the latest news, and be the first to know what Snot Rocket is up to next.

Only at <u>www.ryanstygar.com</u>!

About the Author

Ryan Stygar writes fiction for young readers and adults. Ryan's vision was to create a new hero that used math and science to save the world. Ryan hopes that each *Snot Rocket* adventure will inspire a love of learning in his readers. Ryan currently attends law school at California Western School of Law in San Diego, CA.

About the Illustrator

Garrett Dare is a digital artist and animator. He's produced cartoons, animated commercials, and illustrations. He is currently studying "Art & Technology" at the University of Oregon. His work can be viewed at www.garrettdare.com

Made in the USA
Middletown, DE
04 December 2019